BUDDY AND THE VIRUS

MICHELLE STIMPSON
CASANDRA MCLAUGHLIN

During this time of pandemic
stand on Proverbs 3:5-7.
God truly has us in His hands.

ACKNOWLEDGMENTS

To the only wise, true God - we thank Him for the ability to write, to encourage, and to minister through books that touch the heart. And, always, we thank our readers for their continued support. Thanks to our families who loan us out to this work. We love you all. Take care!

*I*t didn't make any sense to Buddy Wilson how people were running around like chickens with their heads cut off, acting like the sky was falling. Every news channel you turned on, folks was talking about Chronicles. Or was it Coronity? Corona19? Something that sounded like the kind of name someone named their child after losing a bet.

As he waltzed through the elegant lobby of the Magnolia Gardens senior village after a late dinner, all he could see was people watching news channels and scrolling through their phones. The red boxes indicating breaking news seemed to surround him.

"Buddy, you heard the latest?" the receptionist asked him as he casually walked back to his room.

"No. And I don't want to hear. Y'all over-panicking about this thing." He huffed, shaking his head. "How in the world is a virus in China coming all the way across the water in less than a month?"

The brown-haired, blue-eyed woman skewed her head to the side and squinted at him. "Are you serious?"

"Of course, I'm serious. All the news does is make people scared. I, for one, am not buying it. When they shut down the liquor stores and the Bingo houses, then maybe I'll get scared."

"Um...you're actually in a high risk category, Mr. Wilson, being a senior citizen. You might want to rethink your position and learn how you can protect yourself."

Buddy waved her off. "Nonsense. This is all a bunch of foolishness. They just got finished impeaching the President. Then Kobe Bryant and his daughter and a bunch of their friends died... Now that was really sad. But this here virus? This'll blow over soon."

Undaunted, the woman reiterated her warning. And Buddy walked away from her, still wondering exactly how to pronounce the name of all this craziness.

He moseyed on down the hallway toward his fiancé, Bertha's, room and knocked on the door. "Bertha, you in the bed yet?"

Seconds later, she opened the door wearing a satin night gown, fuzzy pink slippers, and a hair bonnet.

Seeing her in next to nothing made Buddy want to hurry up and say his vows. Bertha was a whole lotta woman, and he could hardly wait to make her his wife.

"I was up watching the news," she said.

He noticed her widened eyes, as if she was afraid of something.

"You okay?"

"Yeah. It's just...everything that's going on." She motioned toward the ceiling.

Buddy couldn't help but notice how she jiggled under that thin gown.

Bertha must have taken note, too, because she excused herself for a second, went to the restroom, and came back wearing a terrycloth robe.

"Baby, come on now," Buddy said with a grin. "Don't do me like that."

"No, sir," Bertha said, shaking her hand. "No peep shows here."

Buddy wondered if asking Bertha to marry him had been a mistake. Maybe if he'd just made her his permanent girlfriend, she might not have been still playing hard-to-get in the months leading up to their wedding.

"You can come sit for a while," Bertha said. She moved aside to let Buddy enter her sitting area.

She joined him on the couch. "It's really terrible what's happening in Italy. Schools are closed, people trapped in their own houses, hospitals overcrowded."

Buddy wrinkled his eyebrows. "Italy? I thought it was in China."

"It was. But it's moving across the globe."

"How close is Italy to China?"

She glared at him. "Didn't you take geography in high school?"

Buddy scrunched his face, trying to envision a world map. "Look, I don't remember a whole lot from my history classes, but I know Italy ain't right next to China. So how did it skip over all those other countries and get all the way to Italy?"

Bertha blinked slowly in disgust. "I. Don't. Know. All I know is, it's up in Italy and it's here in America now, and we got a real problem on our hands if we don't do something quick."

"Something like what?"

"Something like get somewhere and be still. Hunker down until it passes."

Buddy tisked. "Woman, you actin' like Cavassas is the angel of death itself."

"It's Coronavirus, and it is for some people. Particularly people like us."

Buddy stood up and stretched his arms. Then he flexed his puny muscles for Bertha. "I'm the picture of health."

Bertha gave a tentative laugh, but her serious scowl quickly returned. She patted for him to sit on the couch again. "I'm serious, Buddy. We all need to stay inside."

Again, Buddy shook his head. "I ain't doin' it. If Coronado comes for me, that'll just be the end."

"It's not that simple," she tried to explain. "It takes a while for you to know you've got it. By then, you could have passed it on to God only knows how many people. That's why *everyone* needs to be careful."

Buddy couldn't believe how serious Bertha's expression was. Her skin crinkled between her eyes, staring at him with all sincerity. Serious as a heart attack.

"Now wait a minute, Bertha. Let's think this through." Buddy counted off on his fingers. "Number one, do you really think the United States is gonna let something like a virus shut everything down? That sounds like something from the 1800s, before we had good sense. Number two, China and Italy ain't America. People do stuff different there. Eat different stuff. They buy food outside over there. In America, all our stuff is good 'n processed."

She leaned away from him. "You actin' like all that processed food is good for us or something. Like having food outside isn't the way folks sold food for centuries before we got all these grocery stores."

"Wait. I'm not finished." Buddy counted on. "Number four."

"Three," Bertha corrected him.

"Three. All the news do is hunt for what'll make people scared. Shoot, they probably just ran out of news to report and had to come up with something quick. You know they can't just say, 'We ain't got no bad news today. Tune in tomorrow. Good night.' Naw, they got to come up with *something* to keep folks paranoid." He tapped his temple. "But they're not fooling me. I'm smarter than that."

"Bud—"

"And last but not least," he continued, "let's say I am at high risk. I got a right to live my life just like everybody else. Matter of fact, since I'm old, I have more of a right to enjoy my last days. I am not going to lock myself in a box for other people. Nosiree. Not over the Cassanova virus."

Bertha peered at him. "Are you serious?"

This was the second time someone had tried to make him feel bad for his bravery.

"Yes ma'am."

Bertha rolled her eyes. "Do you now know that the reason Zeke and Frenchie haven't come back from their cruise is because they can't get off their boat?"

He sucked in his neck. "I thought they were still on the ship."

"They are. They're docked at the port. The health department won't let them off the ship until they are cleared for a certain amount of time."

"How you know?"

"Norman just told me. Said the front desk gave him a message to pray for them."

Buddy vaguely remembered that Zeke and Frenchie were due back a few days ago. He'd just figured they decided to extend their honeymoon a little longer.

"Wait a minute. What are you doing talking to Norman this late at night?"

Bertha reached for her phone and showed him the group text message.

"It's our prayer chain."

He glanced at the screen and saw names he knew from Magnolia Gardens, the senior center they lived in. "How come I ain't on the prayer chain?"

She sighed. "Are you going to pray for Zeke, Frenchie, and the rest of the world during this crisis?"

"It's *not* a crisis," Buddy declared. "It's a fake crisis. For once, I gotta agree with the President. It's too much fake news going around."

Bertha stood. "Good night, Buddy. I can't argue with you tonight."

Buddy stomped out of Bertha's room. *This is what's wrong with women. Always getting their feelings involved.* He wondered if he was ready to live with such an emotional creature again.

When he got back to his room, Buddy opened his flip phone and found his very own message from Zeke.

He smiled. Zeke must have known that Norman wouldn't contact Buddy through the prayer chain, so he'd sent Buddy his own personal text message.

Stuck on ship due to virus. Take care out there. This thing is real.

2

"*I* can't believe you got me up at six o'clock to go stand in line at Wal-Mart," Buddy fussed as he turned into the store's parking lot. To his surprise the lot was packed.

"Now do you understand why I wanted to get here early?" Bertha pointed to the long line of people waiting.

"We can just go to another store. It ain't that serious."

"Wherever we go I'm sure it'll be the same thing. Come on, let's go get in line before it wraps around the building." She opened the door and got out the car before he could respond.

Buddy huffed and followed Bertha who was walking so fast he could hardly keep up with her.

"This don't make no sense. Boy I tell you, the government will find a way to get a few extra dollars."

Bertha eyed him.

But that didn't stop him. "One case of water per person," he said aloud, reading the stores sign. "Now they gon have people scared of a water shortage."

Several people laughed, which encouraged him to continue.

"Who says you have to drink bottled water anyway?

When I was growing up, we drunk sink water, water out of the hose outside, and we made it. Ain't that right?" he asked an older gentleman who looked to be in his 70s.

"Yeah we did, but we're living in a different time now."

"The only time that changes is on the clock and calendar." Buddy waved him off.

By this time Bertha was seething and rocking back and forth.

"Will you please stop?" she mumbled.

"What I do? Where's the lie?

Tell me I'm wrong and I'll be quiet."

"You ain't lying," another shopper chimed in as the line moved up.

He immediately stopped speaking when his wife elbowed him in the side.

Buddy cackled and shook his head.

"You're embarrassing me, and I wish I would have caught a ride with Tracy," Bertha said as they entered the store. She pulled out her wipes and wiped down the basket. She rolled the basket at a high speed, attempting to leave Buddy behind.

They went down two aisles in silence.

"Look, they got your favorite Apple Cinnamon oatmeal," he said, trying to break the ice.

Bertha still didn't say a word.

"Baby, I'm sorry. Don't give me the silent treatment," he pleaded.

Maneuvering the basket around him, she retrieved a few more items and strolled to the other end of the aisle.

Buddy caught up to her and grabbed her arm. "Bertha, I said I'm sorry. What do I have to do for you to forgive me?"

"You can start by not being a clown."

"A clown? I'm just being me."

"Buddy, at some point in your life you've got to start taking things seriously. You're always joking. This ain't nothing to be playing with."

"Bertha, I'm just like the pawn shop; you gotta take me as is." He flashed a smile. "This virus got you all worked up, in your feelings, and overreacting," he added.

"We could die. Why is that so hard for you to understand? Why don't you just wait for me in the car? I don't need your help. I can get my groceries by myself," Bertha spat and rolled away from him.

Just then his cell phone rang.

He opted not to argue with her because that could have possibly made things worse. He was already in trouble.

To Buddy's surprise it was his son calling.

"Chris? Hey, how are things going?"

Buddy found the exit and made his way to the car.

"Pops, I was calling to check on you. Is Magnolia Gardens requesting that you all do shelter in place? Will they allow you to vacate the premises?"

"Vacate for what?" He laughed.

"I'm just saying it would probably be best for you to be here than there."

"And why is that?" Buddy opened the car door and got in.

"This virus is running rapid, and you're in the high risk category. There aren't any cases out here in Blue Bond."

"That's cause ain't nobody living out there but you and maybe three other families."

Blue Bond was 40 miles away from Magnolia Gardens on the outskirts of town. Chris and his wife, Malorie, had built a home out there after he retired from the army.

"I see the news folks got you scared too. How are you a retired Sergeant Major and scared?"

"It's not about being scared, it's about being cautious."

"I refuse to let some bogus Convonta virus run me up out of my comfort zone."

Chris laughed. "It's Corona and it's not bogus. Too many people are dying behind this thing. I just want you to take it seriously." His tone changed and voice lowered a slight bit.

"People are dying from death, if it's they time to go they gon go. That's life, son. I appreciate the offer but I'm just fine," Buddy assured him.

"You know Mal and I have plenty of room if you want to come. I'm sure Cindy would love to see her grandpa. C.J. is home too. We'd of course let you have the guest house. You'd have your own place just like at Magnolia Gardens," Chris pointed out.

"I know C.J. is having a fit being back home especially since he's used to living on campus. When's the graduation?"

"From the looks of things they might not have a graduation ceremony. We'll know for sure in the weeks to come."

"Well at least he'll have his degree and that's all that matters. Let me get off this phone. I got some business to take care of. I'll talk to you again soon," Buddy said as he spotted Bertha heading to the car.

"Alright, Pops. Love you, man."

"Back at you." Buddy disconnected the call and got out the car and popped the trunk.

"Find everything you need?" he asked and began to place the bags in the car.

"There are a few more items I need but I'll just get Tracy to take me to another store later," Bertha said not making eye contact with him.

"Why would you ask Tracy when we're already out?

You still mad? He shut the trunk of the car and got in the driver's seat. "

"Don't you know being mad will shorten your life quicker than the Cavontay virus," he stated once they settled inside the car. "Now tell me where you wanna go."

"I want you to take me home."

"You just said you need a few more things."

"Buddy, look. I don't know if I can do this."

"Do what?"

"Do us," she blurted out. "I don't know if I can be with someone who can't take life seriously."

"So you mean to tell me you're going to let a virus come between us. I can't apologize for not reacting the way you want me to react. I'm not wired like that. I laugh at life before it laughs at me. You want me to be different, act different. Maybe you right. Maybe we can't do us."

That's why I've been by myself all these years. Imma be me point blank period.

Buddy glanced over at Bertha who was purposely ignoring him by looking out the window. He sped the car up and turned the radio on.

3

*B*uddy settled on the couch with a bag of pork skins and a glass of lemonade and decided to call his best friend. "Earnest, man, what y'all doing over there?"

"Not a whole lot. Tracy just ordered Chinese food for dinner."

"Man, don't eat that. She trying to kill you. You know Covona came from China."

"It's Corona." Earnest chuckled. "Besides, I might as well eat it because truthfully we just need to pray over all our food no matter where it comes from. And what are you crunching on?"

"I got me some good ol' pork skins and later on I'm going to eat some American made summer sausage, cheese, and nilla wafers. I'll probably run up to the store and get a few more snacks later on." Buddy continued to smack.

"Tracy and I plan to go get some groceries too especially since the cafeteria won't have extended hours anymore."

"I'm sure she'll get you some Beanie Weenies and every microwavable meal she can find 'cause we all know Tracy can't cook." Buddy snickered.

"Well at least I got a woman to cook for me. You over there all by yourself eating nothing but junk food," Earnest pointed out.

"Anyway, why weren't you on the Zoom meeting call?"

"My phone ain't set up like that."

"That's cause you won't get rid of that flip phone." Earnest laughed.

"All I need my phone to do is dial numbers. If I want to see somebody I'll go visit them," Buddy stated.

"Well from the looks of things it'll be a while before we get to visit anyone."

"All of this stuff will die down soon."

"If we don't die first," Earnest said somberly.

"Hold up. Don't be talking like that. You got it and ain't told nobody? You got covonya?" Buddy said panicky.

"Buddy, calm down. No I don't have it, but we're all getting tested tomorrow because Lily is running a fever."

"Lily got a fever," he said nervously. "I was just

around her the other day in the laundry room. She seemed okay. Normal goofy Lily.

"Her fever spiked to 103.9 overnight, so now they are all being quarantined upstairs in the west wing of the building. Thankfully that wing is being remodeled and there aren't any residents up there. Check your resident newsletter; they slipped them under the door this morning. They have the scheduled time of the testing and other information concerning changes here at the facility."

Buddy jumped up from the couch, rushed over to the door and retrieved his newsletter, and began pacing the floor. He retrieved a paper towel from the kitchen and wiped his brow. He felt his heart rate increasing.

"Buddy you still there?"

"Yeah, yeah, yeah I'm here."

"Are you alright?"

"I'm good," he slowly replied.

"I'm sure Maxine is fine with her trip to see her son and his family being extended. She had her grandbaby on the Zoom meeting with us. Norman is still stuck in San Antonio. He went there for a conference," Earnest explained.

When he didn't get a response back from Buddy, he said, "Hey, what are you doing? You ain't saying nothing."

"Oh, I'm sorry. I heard what you said but I'll call you later." Buddy disconnected the call before Earnest could say good bye.

This thing is serious. You just don't know how much time we got left. If I could go back into time, I'd change so many things. He sighed.

Sitting at the table, Buddy's mind began to travel back into time when he was young, foot loose and fancy free.

It was the summer of 1976 when he'd meet Clarice Jenkins, a tall, dark chocolate skinned, long haired, big boned woman who Buddy feel head over heels in love with. The two meet when Buddy's ship docked in Norfolk Virginia. Buddy and a few of his shipmates went to Roosters, a hole in the wall. Upon arrival, Buddy spotted Clarice sitting with a group of friends at a table. He immediately went over and introduced himself and asked her if she'd like to dance.

The jukebox was blaring Jr. Walker & The All Stars "Shot Gun". Buddy and Clarice did the mashed potato and danced the night away. The two were smitten by one another, so much so that every time Buddy got a pass to go on leave, he would visit Clarice. They spent the next couple of years writing and calling one another. Things were going great until one evening when Buddy was on leave, Clarice announced they were expecting a child.

"I think we should get married before the baby arrives," Clarice said as she placed a plate of fried chicken, butter biscuits, and homemade gravy in front of Buddy.

"Married? Why do we have to complicate things?" Buddy said, sopping his biscuit in the gravy.

"Buddy, I love you and you love me. Why wouldn't we get married?" Clarice pouted.

"I'm just not ready for that."

"Not ready?" Clarice jumped up from the table and got in his face. "You're not ready to build a family with me, but you're ready to play house. What kind of man are you?"

"Clarice, I will take care of you and the baby. I don't understand what the problem is."

"You don't understand what the problem is. The problem is that I am carrying your baby, your seed, and you don't want to do the right thing by giving us the life we both deserve. If you love me like you say you do, marrying me wouldn't be a problem. You're just selfish and I hate I ever meet you." She ran out the room and into her bedroom and slammed the door.

Buddy banged on the door a few times but decided not to plead his case to her. The truth of the matter was that he was afraid of getting married and felt he was too young. Sure he loved Clarice but he wanted to travel the world, live a little, play a little, and then when the time was right settle down. He gathered his hat and coat and went back to the ship.

The next day he tried to contact Clarice but she hung up on him. Weeks went by, months went by, still no word from Clarice. He never heard from her again until their son, Christopher, was born. His heart was broken when he read the back of the picture, Christopher Lawrence Jenkins. He couldn't believe she didn't give him his last name. After Clarice got out of the hospital, Buddy high tailed it back to Norfolk and stayed with Clarice and Christopher for a few weeks. He vowed to make amends, promising to make things between them right. Buddy had even asked to be stationed in Norfolk permanently. Sadly it never happened because a few months later, Clarice was killed in a car accident. She was the first woman to ever have his heart.

A knock on the door disturbed his thoughts.

Buddy peeped through the door and saw Bertha standing at the door with a mask on.

"Woman, what are you doing? We're supposed to be on lockdown," he said backing away from her and back into his apartment.

Following Buddy, Bertha closed the door.

"I know that, but I had to see you. I miss you and if we were married we'd be stranded together. I don't know how long I can go without seeing you." Tears began to form in her eyes.

"It's okay." Buddy extended his arm and slightly patted her back, not really wanting to get too close to her.

"I don't have the virus, the least you can do is hug me," she pleaded. "I don't want to fight anymore."

Hesitantly he pulled her into his arms and held her. She held on as if her life depended on it. She allowed her tears to flow. Buddy held her tighter. He didn't know who needed that hug the most. Bertha or him.

19

4

*H*earing about Zeke, Frenchie, and Lily trapped on the upper floors and finding out that the governor himself had shut down schools and the NBA had postponed their season and Disneyworld itself had shut down before Spring Break put Buddy in a different mood about that there Carotene virus. Not to mention all the big, greedy corporations that were losing billions by the day.

"Any time rich folk start losing money, you better believe it's serious," Buddy told Earnest over the phone.

"I told you," Earnest gloated. "These may be the last days. For real."

Buddy sank deeper into the pillows atop his bed and crossed his arms. All his life, people had been saying these were the "last days." But the sun was still rising every morning and the moon was still shining every night.

The only difference now, seventy-something years into this thing called life, was that Buddy knew for sure his last days were just around the corner. Had to be. And from the looks of the images flashing on TV, where big cities looked like ghost towns, the rest of the world might be right along with him.

"Buddy, you sure quiet. You all right?"

Buddy was getting tired of people asking him that question. Ever since he finally got on the same page with the rest of Magnolia Gardens and the seriousness of the virus hit him, they all claimed his already-skinny face looked a little longer. He wasn't his normal, jovial self.

"I'm fine," Buddy insisted, hoping up from the bed and stretching his arms toward the ceiling, still tucking the phone against his ear. "I just ain't used to being shut in all day. Can't get all my walking in. I'm from the country. I ain't used to all this here sit-still city life."

"We all know you're more country than a syrup sandwich. But you'd better stay put or you gon' be a countrified Coronavirus-havin' case."

Just the fact that, once again, someone was lecturing him sent a streak of rebellion through Buddy. "I gotta go." He snapped his phone shut and walked to the bathroom. Buddy washed his face again just so he'd feel fresh. After toweling off the cold water, he stared at himself in the mirror.

He liked what he saw, despite the wrinkles and nearly-gray beard. Smiling, he said to himself, "Man, you still got it." But the smile quickly faded as a question echoed in his mind: *But how long before you lose it?*

What if, like the people in Italy, he was already positive and just didn't know it yet? What if these were his last weeks on earth? Had he ever told Chris how much he truly loved him? Did Earnest and Zeke know how much he appreciated their friendship? And did Bertha realize how much joy she'd brought to his life?

She was a good woman. Strong and outspoken, but still tender-hearted. And she'd loved him enough to accept that proposal at Zeke and Frenchie's wedding without a ring. Ain't too many women who would say "I do" from the heart, minus the diamond. She deserved better. And he wanted to give it to her while he could because—who knows?—he might be next.

Problem was, the best wasn't in Magnolia Gardens. It was out there. In the streets. He had to do right by Bertha because, pretty soon, she might not have anything to remember him by.

Besides, it couldn't be healthy, breathing all this same air circulating in and out of all the rooms at Magnolia Gardens. Nobody had mentioned recycled air as a health concern.

A horrifying thought hit him: *Maybe it's in the air. In the ducts and vents of the building.*

He vaguely remembered people saying that it was

best to wear a mask out in public.

Quickly, he tumbled through his sock drawer and found a bandana. Buddy tied it around his face. Another glance in the mirror and he realized that he looked like a criminal.

"Lord, if the Colorado virus don't get me, the police will." He laughed to himself.

With that resignation, Buddy peeked out his doorway. Looked left and right. When he saw the coast was clear, he made a dash for the nearest exit and out to the parking lot. He hopped in his car and drove to the one place where he knew the world hadn't stopped.

FORTY MINUTES LATER, Buddy pulled into the parking lot of Big Teddy's Pawn Shop in Broken Fork, TX. Just as Buddy suspected, there were still people out and about. None of them were wearing masks as they waltzed from store to store at the small, off-the-main-roads shopping center, so Buddy decided to leave his bandana in the car. It probably wouldn't be a good idea to go into a pawn shop with a mask on his face anyway. Big Teddy didn't play, and he might not recognize Buddy after all these years.

The electronic chime, the cowbell, and the closed circuit television screen greeted Buddy first upon entrance.

"Hello there," a rowdy male voice called from the back.

At six foot four and four hundred pounds, Big Teddy lived up to his name. But his entrance was obviously painstaking, as he struggled to shift his weight from knee to knee. Buddy felt kind of bad for Big Teddy. Nearly the same age, time was catching up to them both.

"Buddy Wilson," Big Teddy exclaimed. "I do declare. I ain't seen you in years."

Buddy took the recognition as a good sign. "What you been up to, old man?"

Teddy smiled, his blue eyes crinkling up at the corners. "Same old, same old. But right now, tryin' to help folks pay their light bills. This virus got folk off work, tryin' to sell everything they got to keep food on the table. It's bad for the public, but good for me. Except we got reduced hours."

That was more information than Buddy asked for, but he'd expected no less from Big Teddy. Running a pawn shop at the juncture of three small towns, he knew everybody's business, just like his father, Little Teddy, had.

Teddy leaned his elbows on the glass case and eyed Buddy's pockets. "What you wantin' to sell?"

"Oh, no. I'm here to buy," Buddy boasted, pulling up the waist of his britches. "And hopefully the rules of supply and demand will help bring down my price today."

"Achoo," Teddy sneezed. He wiped his nose with

leathery, age-spotted hands. Then he squirted his hands with hand sanitizer from a giant bottle sitting on the corner of the main glass case.

Buddy was thankful to see Big Teddy's concern for health.

"I got me a woman," Buddy announced to Big Teddy and the two other people in the store who were shopping for computers.

"Is that so?" Teddy sneezed again and repeated his quick hand-cleaning gesture.

Buddy paid close attention to Big Teddy's face now. His nose was a little red. Eyes watery.

"Do you have the Cova19 virus? "You all right?"

"Aww yea." Big Teddy swatted the air. "Just allergies. Say you got a woman, huh? She real pretty, I bet. You always did have the ladies chasing after you."

Buddy snickered. "You an honest man. That's why I came to you."

After about twenty minutes of showing the rings, reminiscing about the good old days, and haggling for the lowest price, Buddy walked out of Big Teddy's with a solitaire wedding ring. Nothing too fancy, as Bertha didn't like making a big fuss out of things. But enough to let every man at Magnolia Gardens and every dude in the whole wide world know that this woman was taken.

As soon as Big Teddy rang up the transaction and the receipt printed, he fell into a coughing spell so hard he had to take a drink of water from the bottle beneath the cash register.

Buddy had been around folk with allergies before. They didn't do all this kind of crazy coughing like Big Teddy was doing.

With the quickness, Buddy signed for Bertha's ring and left the store. And all the way back to Magnolia Gardens, he was careful not to touch his face because, soon enough, Bertha's lips would be touching his face instead.

5

*B*uddy tossed and turned all night worrying about the coronavirus. Today he was getting tested. With sweat dripping down his face he made his way to the bathroom.

Looking at his face in the mirror, he shook his head in disappointment.

The lines and wrinkles on his face told of the most incredible journey. His eyes told of laughter, of warm smiles and affection. His forehead told of worries past and present. His past was full of the worst memories any life can offer—war and loss. Where had the time gone?

A light cough escaped him.

He attempted to clear his throat.

He coughed several more times.

What if I got it?

What if this is the end?

I've had a good life.

May not have gotten everything right but indeed a good life.

You live and then you die.

Yep that's how the ball bounces.

But I don't wanna die, I got some more living to do.

What about me and Bertha?

He began to panic.

He sat on the toilet and looked towards the ceiling and began to pray.

Lord, I know I ain't been right, I been trying to get better. I read the Bible sometimes so I know it says that if I confess my mess ups You'll clean me up. I hope it ain't too late for You to clean me up. I hope it ain't too late to ask for forgiveness. Please forgive me for running through women, I wanna do things right with Bertha if I get a chance to. Forgive me for gambling and playing those pick 3s. Imma try to get that out my system. Please, just give me another chance. Amen.

Buddy got up from the toilet, turned the sinks faucet on, grabbed his towel, and washed his face and brushed his teeth. His testing time was 9:00 a.m. and he only had 15 minutes to get dressed and go. He hurriedly found a pair of jogging pants and a t-shirt to throw on. All the residents had been given a set time to arrive at the testing center on the 4th floor to keep down traffic and to comply with the social distancing order.

Buddy slowly walked down the hall with his mask on

and a pair of gloves. When he arrived at the elevator, he felt his heart racing.

Calm down. Get yourself together. He gave himself a pep talk.

Stepping off the elevator, he took a deep breath and made his way to the doctor's office which was now set up as the testing center.

A man with a respirator mask, safety glasses, face shield, scrubs, a long sleeved gown, safety gloves, and an apron met him at the door.

"Are you Mr. Buddy Wilson?"

Buddy nodded his head. Seeing the man dressed in this manner increased his nervousness.

"I'm Dr. Moore. I'll be doing your test today. Follow me."

Buddy followed him to the exam room.

"Please have a seat on the exam table."

"What exactly are you planning to do?

Are you taking blood from me?"

"No, Mr. Wilson. This isn't a blood test. Today we're doing what we call a Molecular test?"

"Say what now?"

"We're doing a Molecular test. It is a test that looks for signs of an infection."

Buddy began to really panic as he thought about the coughing spell he'd had earlier.

"Ummmm how long will this take?"

"It won't take long. I'm going to take a sample from

your nose with a cotton swab. Then we'll send it off to be tested."

"How long will it take for me to know if I got Corontig?"

"I think you mean the Coronavirus." Dr. Moore laughed. "We'll have the results in two days. Since you all are in the high risk category, we have to get the results back STAT. Do you have any more questions you'd like to ask before we get started?"

"Naw, I'm good. Let's just get it over with."

Dr. Moore performed the test and told Buddy that someone would contact him in the next few days with the results. He also gave Buddy a pamphlet about the Coronavirus.

By the time Buddy left the testing center, his head was spinning. He made it back to his apartment and watched *The Love Boat* marathon. Bertha would normally be by his side watching TV with him. Buddy loved snacking and was known for making sandwiches and root beer floats, but today, he was so worried that he didn't have an appetite. His phone rang several times but he didn't answer. Didn't feel like talking to anybody. He sat on the couch and picked up the Bible Bertha had given him last year as a birthday gift. When he opened it, he landed on Isaiah 41. Buddy read and when we got to verse 10, he read aloud.

"So do not fear, for I am with you; do not be dismayed, for I am your God. I will strengthen you and help you; I will uphold you with my righteous right hand." Buddy read it again and again. He'd heard the others talk about reading a scripture and meditating on it. This scripture was tugging at him and giving him comfort.

I won't be fearful.

I know you will strengthen me.

I know you will help me.

I know you got me.

He kept reciting those words to himself until he fell asleep on the couch.

6

*B*reakfast didn't start until 7:00 a.m., so it was quite unclear to Buddy why somebody was knocking on his door at 6:38 a.m. There was no alarm, so it couldn't have been a fire drill. And nobody was making social visits, so it couldn't have been Bertha.

"Mr. Wilson," a muffled voice called.

Buddy dug both fists into his couch cushion and pushed himself to a standing position. "Just a second." His muscles and joints hadn't quite warmed up yet, which caused him to shuffle a little slower.

He opened his door. Nobody. *What in the world?*

He looked to his right and saw Manny, one of the cafeteria staff members, knocking on the next door and calling Bob Densmore's name just as he had called Buddy's' only a few moments ago.

Manny, whose nose and mouth were covered by a

white mask, pointed at the brown paper sack at Buddy's feet. "We're serving all meals in your room until further notice. This morning's breakfast is a bacon wrap and apple juice."

A shockwave coursed through Buddy. This was all happening so fast. "Wait? What you sayin'? I got the virus?" *How come they told Manny before telling me?*

"No, sir."

Bob opened his door at that moment, and Manny stepped across the hall to address them both. "Everyone's having their food served in their room. Someone at Magnolia Gardens has tested positive."

Oh, Lord. It's me.

Manny's lips kept moving, but Buddy didn't hear whatever else he said.

Bob picked up his sack, smiled, and said something to Manny.

Buddy didn't hear that, either.

The clock just struck eleven. Buddy swallowed hard. He bent down and picked up his own sack, wondering how long it would take before the staff nurses would come dressed in hazmat gear and escort him to the fourth floor.

It hadn't been 24 hours since his test, though. What exactly had Dr. Moore said yesterday? Did he say the results would be back in a few days or did he give an exact time and date? Shoot, Buddy couldn't remember. All he could do was hope he wasn't the one.

Manny didn't offer any other information. He was already on to the next resident.

Buddy closed the door and plopped down on the couch again and sat the sack on the empty cushion to his right. He didn't have to open it to know what was inside —eggs, bacon, and cheese inside a tortilla wrapped in white paper. Not his favorite. He didn't have an appetite for that quickly assembled, generic wrap for breakfast. Not when he was used to choosing his entree, his juice, and his favorite flavor of jelly.

Bertha liked those wraps. He'd save it and give it to her. Maybe he'd give her the ring today instead of in a few weeks when Zeke and Frenchie got off the fourth floor.

But on second thought, he might not live that long.

And if this was one of these last days, he sure didn't want to spend them eating nasty breakfast wraps. Alone. Would God do him like this? After all, Buddy had offered his soul for some good years with Bertha.

Maybe God doesn't want these last, leftover, rickety years from me. Maybe he had hurt too many women, gambled away one too many gifts, waited one day too late. Really, Buddy wouldn't blame God. Don't nobody want the last dregs of life.

"Well, God, I understand if you don't want to fool with me," Buddy said to the One he had often referred to as The Man Upstairs. God probably didn't like being called by that name, come to think of it. Buddy couldn't blame Him for that, either. He deserved so much more than a name somebody might call their tenant or someone sharing their house.

Buddy wondered why all of this was occurring to him now. Why this sudden understanding of Who God really is was hitting him in ways that had not occurred to him in his whole, entire life. Honestly, he felt like crying.

Absentmindedly, Buddy reached into the paper bag and went ahead and started eating the wrap despite it not being his favorite. Not because he was hungry, but because it might be hours before Manny or someone else from the cafeteria came by with a lunch tray. The few snacks Buddy had to tide him over between meals certainly needed to be rationed right now.

His phone rang and, quickly, Buddy snatched his cheerful voice back into place to answer. "Chelllllll-o?"

"Buddy, did you hear?" Bertha's frantic voice squeaked.

"Hear what?"

"It's Lily. She's positive for the Coronavirus."

Buddy gasped. "Aww naw."

Buddy had never been so troubled and relieved at the same time. Trouble because Lily was in danger, but relieved he wasn't positive. At least not for now. As quickly as he had that mixture of thoughts, his conscience began to taunt him. *You shole ain't no Christian, thinking selfish thoughts like that.*

This voice—the ridicule in his mind—was more like

what he was used to than the one that had been trying to help him grasp who God is.

Bertha continued, "They said she's doing fairly well, though. Norman is going to do a televised prayer for her later this morning. You can tune in if you want."

"How?"

"Didn't you read the note in your breakfast bag?"

Buddy reached into the bag and pulled the note out. With Bertha still on the phone, he read the correspondence out loud.

MAGNOLIA GARDENS FAMILY,

It is with sincere concern for our community that we relay news that one of our own has contracted the virus. Lily Jones has bravely decided to let everyone know that she is battling this virus courageously and is doing quite well despite a loss of appetite and general fatigue. She welcomes your prayers and well wishes.

Management at Magnolia Gardens is working to keep you safe and healthy until this situation passes by. Many of us have lived through worse, and we will make it through this together as well. For now, please relax and remain in your rooms until we are able to take extensive disinfecting measures to ensure that our facility is safe for everyone to participate in limited activities.

Thanks to technology, Pastor Norman Walker will be able to conduct a prayer this afternoon on our closed circuit channel (17) today at 8:00 a.m. All are welcome to tune in if you would like.

Sincerely,

Your Magnolia Gardens Management Family

"YOU GONNA WATCH NORMAN?" Bertha asked.

"Yeah," Buddy said. "Of course."

"Well, all right," Bertha said tentatively. "You've just been acting so weird lately. And don't think I don't know about you leaving the building the other day. What was so important you had to possibly bring another starting point for the virus at Magnolia Gardens?"

"I-I-it was just…" Buddy trailed off.

"A lottery ticket, right?" Bertha accused.

"It's still a free country," Buddy said.

Bertha sighed. "I suppose it is, Buddy. But I'd really, really like to have you living in it with me."

Buddy smiled. "Yeah. I feel the same way. I won't get out anymore until it's safe. I promise."

"I'm so glad to hear that, baby."

They exchanged a few more sweet nothings before hanging up. Buddy turned on his television and found channel 17, which he didn't even know was available on their system. Buddy wondered what other channels might be available. And since there was still quite some time before the broadcast, he decided to surf around the channels.

That's when he stumbled upon someone who looked quite familiar. A preacher dressed in jeans and a plain black T-shirt stood on a simple stage with a microphone. His name was displayed at the bottom of the screen—Heathcliff Ride, III. Unlike most of the other bootleg televangelists Buddy was used to seeing, there was something sincere about the man's brown eyes coupled with the lack of fanfare on screen.

"You. Right there. Watching this broadcast," the preacher said, pointing his finger directly at the camera.

Suddenly, Buddy felt as though he were staring at Uncle Sam's "I Want You" poster. No matter where you turned, the finger was pointing at you.

The preacher continued, "I want you to know God loves you. No matter what you've done, no matter how far you've gone, no matter how long you stayed gone. God loved you then as much as He loves you right now. Don't let the enemy talk you out of God's love. Amen?"

From deep down within himself, Buddy breathed a sigh of relief and agreed, "Amen."

By the time Norman came on with his prayer for Lily, Buddy was more than ready to hear more good news from heaven.

He could use all the good news available to tide him over until the doctor's report came in.

7

*B*uddy was determined to get some fresh air today. He felt great after last night's prayer call but his mind was still on his test results. Dr. Moore had told him he'd have his results today. He was sure that he had the virus especially since Lily tested positive.

As he walked the trail at Magnolia Gardens, he replayed the last time he was around Lily.

The two were doing laundry and Buddy remembered seeing Lily and speaking to her but not being too close to her. She was on the opposite side of the room and in a hurry to get her clothes so that she wouldn't be late for pottery class.

Maybe the virus traveled across the room.

Maybe she sneezed and touched the door handle.

They probably gave me the virus when they stuck that darn swab down my throat.

I should have known not to trust the government.

Trust me...

Buddy turned around to see if someone was behind him.

I must be hearing things.

Trust me...

The voice said again.

He had heard Norman say several times that you could hear the voice of God. Never in a million years did he think he would experience it.

Suddenly the overcast of the clouds was interrupted by the sun giving him a sense of peace.

"Thank you, God," he whispered.

The buzz from his jacket pocket startled him. He pulled his phone out his pocket and almost dropped it.

"Hello."

"Pops, how you doing?"

"Hey, son. I'm doing great. How are y'all doing out there?"

"We're doing great but I'm concerned about you. I just saw on the news that one of the residents there has the virus. Do you know the person?"

"Yea. Lily is a friend of mine."

"I'm sorry to hear that. Did you get tested?" Christopher asked with a concerned tone.

"I was tested and I get my results today, but I'm not worried. I don't have it," Buddy said with confidence.

"I really wish you would just come stay with us."

"I would like that but I can't leave my lady friend," Buddy said, making his way to the patio bench.

"Oh I didn't know you were seeing someone. If she was your wife she'd be more than welcome to come and stay. I can't promote shacking around my kids."

Buddy was proud to hear his son talk about doing what's right. He certainly hadn't taught him that. Chris had spent his childhood with his Aunt Emma and Uncle Larry. Buddy only saw him when he was on leave. The military made sure that he took care of his financial responsibility and Buddy made sure he spent as many holidays as he could with him so he could have somewhat of a relationship with his son. Chris went into the military right after high school and lived some of his time overseas. After he married, he was stationed back in the states and found Buddy. Since then, the two became close and vowed to stay in touch with one another.

"I wouldn't ask you to do that. For the record, I plan to marry her when all of this is over. It's time for your old man to settle down."

"I'm happy for you. Hopefully this will be over soon and you guys can come for a back yard barbeque."

"Sounds good. I'm looking forward to it. In fact I think we should start spending more time together anyway. You're not getting any younger." Buddy chuckled.

"Don't you mean you're not getting any older?" Chris laughed.

"Anyway, I better get off this phone. I've got to go get my results."

"Call me as soon as you know."

"I will. Love you, son."

"Love you, too, Pops. Take care of yourself."

Buddy placed his mask on his face and went inside the building.

"I trust You, God," he said as he took the elevator to the doctor's office.

Dr. Moore greeted him and Buddy followed him to the exam room.

"Give it to me straight, doc," Buddy said.

"Well, Mr. Wilson, your results came back and you don't have the coronavirus but you do have a sinus infection.

Here's a prescription for some amoxicillin. Take it as instructed and it should clear up in a few days."

Buddy jumped to his feet, thanked Dr. Moore, and hurriedly left the office. Back in his room, he bowed his head and prayed.

"Lord, thank You for giving me another chance. I'll try not to mess it up and I'm going to make things right with me and Bertha. In Jesus name. Amen."

Eager to make things right with Bertha, he began to think of ways he could propose to her. Bertha often complained that he wasn't romantic enough. He decided to go old school and write her a letter. During his military days, that's how he got the ladies. Buddy laughed at the thought of mail day in the military. His friends would get jealous because he had ladies from different states writing him.

"I can't help if they want to take a deep in this pool," he'd brag to them and stick his chest out as if he was man of the year.

"Those days are over," he declared.

Buddy went to his desk drawer and retrieved his pad and pen.

Dear Bertha,

These past few days, I have been thinking about my future. This virus has made me realize that I shouldn't take things for granted. Mainly you. You have been nothing but patient with me. I never thought I would ever want to settle down until I fell in love with you. I don't want to waste any more time being apart, and I can't imagine life without you. I thank you for putting up with me. I'm asking that you put up with me until our days end. What I'm trying to say is, will you be the cool in my whip? Will you be the sugar in my kool- aid? Will you be the ice to my cream? Will you be the almond to my joy? Will you be my wife, Bertha? I love you.

P.S. I'm Coronvid Free, Baby!

Yours Forever, Buddy

Satisfied with what he'd written, Buddy folded the note, placed it in an envelope, sealed it, and wrote: *To My Sugar Bunny* on the front of it. He then got the ring box and placed the note and the ring inside a small plastic bag.

He snuck out of his room, took the bag, and went to Bertha's. With his gloved hand, he placed the bag on her door knob, knocked, and sprinted down the hall back to his room.

8

THREE WEEKS LATER

*a*s it turned out, the Orchid county courthouse was open by appointment for marriage licenses. Buddy had done his homework. He was ready the day that he and Bertha made the trip.

He wore a mask, gloves, goggles, a scarf, baseball cap, and a pair of boots with his denim overalls and plaid, long sleeved shirt. All of this despite the warm spring temperatures.

"Buddy. Really?" Bertha questioned him when she met him at the back door.

"I ain't takin' no chances," he barely managed to say through his 4-ply cloth mask. "Magnolia Gardens got a lucky streak. Ain't but a few residents got Cavalier virus, and every last one of them recovered. I don't want to be the one to break the record."

Bertha shook her head and laughed. "I give up on two

things with you today. The correct name, and trying to convince you that all this you got on is not necessary." She looked down at his side pocket. "What's in there?"

"Hand sanitizer," he said. He patted the other side. "Got Clorox wipes in here, too. Matter of fact, let me wipe down this handle before we press it." Quickly, he whipped out a white wipe and sanitized the rectangular push-bar.

"I wasn't planning on pressing with my hand, Buddy. I always use my body for these types of doors," Bertha declared.

"That might be worse, for all we know." He pushed the door open and tossed the wipe in the trash bin right outside. Bowing and with an extended arm, he said, "After you, my love."

"You gonna keep all this on in the car, too?" Bertha asked.

"Ain't no need in taking it off."

And he meant just that. Buddy kept all his gear intact all the way to the county courthouse. He wiped off every door handle, the numbers on the elevator, the rails inside the elevator, the pen they used to sign in, and the seats they waited in before their number was called.

"Thank you, sir," total strangers told him.

"My pleasure," he responded with a nod. But he didn't breathe again until he was at least 10 feet away from the people thanking him. Buddy had a new lease on life, and he wasn't going to take chances on other people's foolishness. Granted, he had once been foolish himself. Not just about the virus, but about life, period. Not any more, though. He had a good woman, a good son, good friends, and a good God. That was a lot more than he even knew to hope for until now.

Another good thing about this day was the fact they only had to wait five minutes before they were called back to the window.

"First time I ever waited in line for the government this short a time," Buddy said under his breath.

"Mmm hmm," Bertha agreed. "They need to make appointments all the time."

She directed her attention to the woman behind the Plexiglas counter. Her name badge read *Karissa*. "We're here for our nine o'clock appointment to get our marriage license. Buddy and Bertha."

Karissa blinked with surprise. "You two?"

Buddy put an arm around Bertha's shoulder. "Yes, ma'am. *Us* two. And we ain't got forever to wait, as you can see." For good measure, he kissed Bertha's cheek despite the masks they were both wearing.

The woman blushed and quickly looked at her computer screen. "Oh. Certainly. Okay. Yes sir. And ma'am."

Bertha nudged Buddy in the side and whispered, "Quit embarassin' people."

"She the one ought to be embarrassed. This is age discrimination," he murmured, but not loud enough so as

47

to cause further discomfort for the lady. Really, falling in love and getting married had come as a surprise to him, too. He supposed it was all right for other people to feel the same way. Especially young people. They always think senior citizens are supposed to sit in rocking chairs and watch the news all day. But not him. Not Bertha. Very few people at Magnolia Gardens lived that lifestyle, in fact.

"I'll need to see your IDs."

Bertha and Buddy handed them to Karissa.

She punched a few buttons and said, "Looks like you filled out everything else online. That'll be eighty-two dollars."

Buddy gave his credit card and the transaction was complete in a jiffy.

Karissa tried to give the IDs and credit card back to Bertha, but before Bertha could take them back, Buddy snatched the two licenses from Karissa and wiped them with a disinfecting towel.

"Can't be too cautious," he said.

Bertha rolled her eyes. "Forgive him."

"It's okay," Karissa said. "He's right. I'm not in a high risk group, but I do need to be more careful. And so do y'all. I mean, I can't imagine you're not having a gathering for the wedding, are you?"

"Oh no," Buddy said.

Karissa shrugged. "So what's the rush on the license?"

Bertha raised her eyebrows. "We're very much in love and we just wanna do things right. Tie the knot."

"Yeah," Buddy added, "she's knocked up. I'm tryna marry her before the baby gets here."

Karissa's green eyes bugged out so far, Buddy had to stop himself from laughing so hard or else he would nullify the effects of his mask. He slapped his knees. "Whew! I gotcha there, didn't I?"

Karissa laughed, too. "I...um..."

Bertha shook her head. "Don't mind him, sweetheart. He's a part-time comedian. We got plans for a ceremony, though. And we need this license to make them happen. Thank you so much."

Karissa stepped away to get the license from a printer.

Buddy stood at the counter laughing at his own joke again every few seconds

Bertha finally joined in. "What am I going to do with you?"

"I don't know, but we're sure gonna have a lot of fun together finding out."

When Karissa came back, she congratulated them again. "I wish you two the best of luck. You remind me of my grandparents. They were married for, like, sixty years."

"That's a blessing," Bertha said.

Once again, Buddy intercepted and took the manila envelope from Karissa.

Bertha stopped him cold with a hand on his wrist.

"Buddy, you can't wipe this down. You'll get it all wet and ruin the license."

"I got a plan." He produced an enormous plastic Ziploc bag and placed the envelope as carefully as a police officer collecting evidence from a crime scene.

The smile on Bertha's face said she hadn't expected him to come through like that. Priceless.

"Buddy, just when I think I've figured you out, you go and change on me."

He winked at his bride-to-be. "Sometimes, a change is good."

She agreed. "It sure it, honey. Sure is."

SEVENTY-TWO HOURS LATER, Buddy was tightening a tie against his neck, spritzing cologne on his lapel, and fastening his cufflinks.

It was time for his and Bertha's big moment.

Her knock, the only one he was expecting, came at nine o-clock on the dot.

Buddy opened the door and beheld his bride. Her mahogany skin was the perfect contrast to her ivory, lacy dress. The front part had just enough plunge in the neckline to show off Bertha's curves. Good thing he was the only one who was going to see them up front and personal, otherwise he might have to fight off some of them flirty ones at Magnolia Gardens.

"Bertha, you are breathtaking," he said.

"You ain't too bad yourself," she said, smiling back at him.

He leaned in for a kiss, but Bertha wasn't having it. "Not until after we're pronounced man and wife."

"Aww, girl, come on."

"Buddy." She stamped her pearl-laced shoes. "I don't think so."

"Fine." He huffed playfully. "How do we get this ceremony going, then?"

Bertha heaved her dress up as she waltzed to his television. "First, turn it on the internal channel."

Seconds later, their closest acquaintances appeared on the screen. Zeke and Frenchie, Lily, Tracey and Earnest, Chris and his wife, Malorie, Norman, Bertha's cousin Lil' Bit, and a few other Magnolia Gardens residents.

"They look like the Brady Bunch," Buddy remarked. "All in their little squares on the same screen."

"It's a Zoom meeting, Buddy," Bertha informed him. "A Zoom wedding, actually."

Buddy had never heard of such a thing in all his life, but as soon as Bertha pushed some buttons on her phone, he and Bertha were in the middle of the screen as well, and everyone started Ooohing and aaaahing about Bertha's dress.

"You look so beautiful," Tracey exclaimed. "Turn around, girl."

Bertha gave her camera to Buddy. "Here, baby, hold it, while I show everyone my dress."

Buddy took the phone and turned it toward himself, which caused a fuss.

"We don't want to see your mug, Buddy."

"Point the camera toward Bertha," they hollered.

"I am," Buddy said.

"No, you aren't," Lily informed him.

Bertha took the phone from him, positioned him with his arm in the air, the camera angled down at her, and told him not to move.

Again, the faces in the squares on the screen fawned over Bertha.

Standing there, watching his beautiful bride twirl in all her glory, made Buddy's throat tighten. She was, indeed, beautiful from the inside out.

Quickly, he lowered his hand to wipe a tear from his eye which, of course, messed up their view of Bertha.

"Buddy," their guests yelled. "What are you doing?"

Bertha faced him again and then froze. Her face melted with emotion. "Oh, Buddy. Don't cry."

"Awwww," came from the television in unison.

"Oh, she got you now," Earnest yelled. "You all the way smitten, man."

The fellows teased, but Buddy didn't care. This was one of the best days of his life.

"Shall we begin?" Norman asked.

Drying his eyes, Buddy said, "Yes, sir."

And right there, in the virtual presence of their Magnolia Gardens and extended families, Buddy said "I

Do" to the one woman who had captured his heart during his golden years. He didn't know how many of those years he had left, but he couldn't think of a better way to spend them than with Bertha and their Magnolia Gardens family.

WANT MORE OF BUDDY & THE MAGNOLIA GARDENS FAMILY?

Here's an excerpt from Chapter 1 of Step of Faith - Book 1 in the Magnolia Gardens Series! Get all three books in the series online now!

* * *

This used to be the best day of the year. Family, friends, food, gifts. Sometimes even singing, if her husband's arthritic fingers allowed him to tickle the ivories through a verse of Silent Night.

The kids used to wake up before sunrise to open their gifts. And, of course, Frenchetta Davenport would barely sleep the night before. She and Elroy might have stayed up half the night, with him assembling toys and her cooking for a scrumptious breakfast and belt-busting lunch. Entertaining and making memories in their fifty-five hundred square-foot home had been the joy of Frenchetta's life.

"Frenchie, you've outdone yourself," people would remark, rubbing their stomachs. Some of them even asked to spend a few hours sleeping in the guest room before they hit the road. Of course, Frenchetta was happy to oblige their requests. People needed her hospitality, her kindness. They benefited from her cooking and housekeeping skills. For Frenchetta, there was no greater purpose in life than those kinds of days.

But this Christmas Day, none of her skills were needed. Elroy was gone. Three Christmases had passed since his sudden hearth attack.

The kids had told her it was too hard to come back home now that their father was dead. "It's just not the same," Katrina said over the phone that first year.

Keith hadn't even bothered to call until after dark. And he sounded drunk on the other end of the line. "Momma, I'll come by tomorrow."

"What are you doing now?" Frenchetta had badgered him.

"I'm at my girlfriend's house."

"Well, you can come by when you finish over there, right?"

Keith hesitated. Sniffed. "I can't. I just can't."

The first Christmas, Frenchetta had understood. The kids were devastated. The second Christmas, she'd managed to talk them into coming over for breakfast at least. She made their favorites—cranberry scones for Katrina, chocolate chip pancakes for Keith. She'd even made French toast for Katrina's twins, though they were barely old enough to chew solid food.

All that food went to waste, however, because nobody came. Nobody. Instead, they had sent text messages with lame excuses for why they weren't coming.

So, this Christmas Frenchetta didn't bother with

cooking or even asking. She'd read an article in a senior magazine about letting go and letting your adult kids make decisions about how they wanted to spend their holidays. She wasn't supposed to try to manipulate or guilt-trip her kids into spending holidays with her. The article assured her that adult children were reasonable and would eventually see the value of aged wisdom in their lives and their children's lives. "It's the circle of life," the article had said. "Humans are wired for multi-generational connection."

Well, if that was true, then Frenchetta's children must be aliens. They could go weeks and months without seeing or speaking to her.

Except, of course, when they needed money. Katrina was married, but she and her husband struggled to pay their bills from time to time. And Keith... *Lord, help.* He was still chasing dreams. He'd even changed his name to LaJermaine and insisted that she refer to him by this new name—unless she was writing out a check to him.

Forget that stupid article. Frenchetta could call Keith and work her way into a conversation about his need for money. He'd come some time in the next few days.

The phone rang, sending Frenchetta's heart racing. She didn't glance at the small blue wording on the phone's console because it was Christmas Day and she wanted some sort of surprise.

Somebody loves me.

"Hello! Merry Christmas!" she answered cheerfully.

The pause should have been her first clue that something was wrong. "Hello. This is Dixon's Pharmacy calling regarding…"

Frenchetta didn't need to listen to the automated call. Tears strolled down her cheek as she pressed the number one to refill her monthly supply of her high cholesterol medication.

"Press pound to confirm your refill."

For a split moment, Frenchetta thought about not pressing the pound button. *What does it matter if I'm well or not?*

Her index finger hovered over the button for a second longer before she gave herself a quick pep talk. "Thank God you're still alive, Frenchie. Healthy, wealthy, wise."

She pushed the button, ensuring that her life-saving medication would be available for pick-up the next day.

But the whole incident scared her. She wasn't exactly suicidal; she just didn't have a huge reason to live. Nothing to look forward to. Unlike her friends who constantly posted pictures at their grandchildren's birthday parties and family vacations on social media, Frenchetta didn't have a close relationship with her adult children.

Come to think of it, she wouldn't have described her relationship with them as "close" even when they were younger. She loved them, of course, from the very beginning. *How could she not?* She and Elroy had no children for the first nine years of their marriage. Then, all of a sudden, her prayers were answered and they suddenly had two.

On top of that, she loved Elroy, and the kids were perfect little representations of their love for one another. Both had Elroy's deep brown skin and Frenchetta's "rabbit" nose. Katrina's little hands mirrored her mother's even from birth, and Keith grew into the spitting image of his father as he approached twenty. Handsome, distinguished-looking.

Elroy worked hard in city administration and business consulting, securing the family's wealth and reputation in Orchid Falls. The Davenports had been the picture-perfect well-off clan. Private schools, vacations abroad, a summer home in Virginia while the kids were growing up.

None of that mattered now. Frenchetta didn't regret putting her kids in all those extracurricular activities or making them participate in the cotillions and the talent competitions. That's what every black family who could afford it did for their kids. They were trying to catch up for generations of setbacks and oppression. Education was the great equalizer, and it was important to project an image that proclaimed, "We are just as good as anyone else."

But Frenchetta wondered now, sitting alone in the lavish decor of her custom-built home, if it had been worth it all. Pushing the kids to perfection, keeping up with the Joneses, teaching them the "importance" of appearing in control at all times. "Never let people see you sweat. That'll make them think you're weak."

Maybe she should have let them sweat. And cry. And be imperfect, even while black. Maybe, then, they would have had some kind of feelings about her. Maybe they would have cared enough to come see about their lonely sixty-year-old mother on Christmas Day.

Frenchetta unbraided her single braid and tussled her long, graying brown hair. This wavy hair had been her signature for as long as she could remember. The full mane was a perfect complement to her small frame, which had made her one of Elroy's greatest prides.

A lot of good my looks are doing me now.

The phone rang again. This time, Frenchetta checked to see who was calling, so as not to get her hopes up.

The caller ID showed 'Gloria Young,' Frenchetta's friend from her days at Hopewell Church.

"Hey, Frenchie! Merry Christmas!"

Frenchetta could hear the rumble of Gloria's family members in the background. "Hey, Glo. Merry Christmas to you, too."

"You all right, Frenchie?"

Frenchetta winced. She hadn't done a very good job of following her own advice because, obviously, Glo had picked up on the distress. "Well, you know. Another Christmas without the kids or my grandkids."

"Where is everybody?"

"Who knows? They haven't called."

"It's only one o'clock. Maybe they'll get in touch later." Gloria suggested.

"I ain't holding my breath." Frenchetta sighed.

"Why don't you come on over here with us," Gloria said. "We've got plenty of food."

"Oh no. I don't want to intrude," Frenchetta declined.

"You're not intruding, I'm inviting you," Gloria said. "In fact, I insist."

"You insist?" Frenchetta laughed. "Girl, you are funny."

"I'm serious, Frenchie. You and I are barely sixty years old. It ain't time to pack up yet. Come on over. Jake made those cookies you like, and I think we're going to go over to see Emma and Paul later. Their senior living place is having an 80s Christmas dance tonight—can you believe that?"

"Oh wow," Frenchetta remarked. "I guess they're living it up in there, huh?"

"I told you. If it were up to me, I'd be there in a heartbeat. But you know Jake. He wants a place to call his own."

"Yeah."

"But there's nothing holding *you* back from moving to one of those places," Gloria added. "Might do you some good. I know you'd have a blast at the Christmas dance!"

For the first time, Frenchetta seriously considered Gloria's words. Like Jake, she'd always had her sights set on owning a piece of America. But today—when that piece seemed so lonely—what was it worth?

"You coming over, girl?"

Frenchetta stood and examined her pale reflection in the mirror. *Good Lord, I need some sunlight.* "Yeah, I guess so."

"That's my Frenchie. You've got a lot of life left to live, girl!"

Frenchetta smiled, thinking Gloria had no idea how timely her statement was.

Books 1 - 3 of the Magnolia Gardens Series are Available Now!

Made in the USA
Las Vegas, NV
09 January 2021

15609450R00042